# Enemies
## and
# Friends

Peter Marney

ISBN-13: 978-1976344374
ISBN-10: 1976344379

This book is dedicated to those
who keep trying, no matter what.

# Read this first

You are not a ninja.

It's very important that you keep remembering this.

If you try to copy any of the stuff in this book then you might end up in hospital.

Even if you copy just some of this stuff, you'll end up in trouble.

This will be bad.

This will be very bad because I'll get the blame.

So please, remember you're not a ninja and promise not to try and copy me.

Have you promised?

Ok, you can now read on.

# My new Dad

I'm back in the middle of a bush and trying very hard to be a leaf. Just a normal leaf that nobody wants to look at today.

Why am I being a leaf?

I'll tell you in a minute.

I got thrown in here by my Dad who I thought was gone forever and who might be if we get discovered.

I'm Jamie by the way. I'm ten years old and this sort of thing doesn't usually happen to me. Ok, maybe it happens a bit more than normal but that's because I'm a Red Sock Ninja although I'm not being much of a ninja at the moment.

I'm being attacked by twigs because the man we're supposed to be following has decided to look for us instead.

Actually we're hoping that he's just being careful and not really looking for a big hairy man and a forgettable ten year old boy.

Being forgettable should be a help when you're following someone but it doesn't seem to be working at the moment.

Dad has just whispered to me to be quiet as our friend might have a gun.

What?!!

Sorry, but this sort of thing isn't supposed to happen in real life. It's ok in a kids' spy book or on the telly but I really don't want to be hunted by someone with a real gun with real bullets which really might hurt me.

Thanks to Keira, I know how to stay silent and frozen and Dad must have had the same lessons because our scary man has lost interest in us and wandered off.

Dad has lost interest as well which is why we're now heading back into the town centre and a promised chocolate milk shake to go inside an already shaken me. The threat of being shot seems to do that to me I've just discovered.

It was supposed to be a quiet chat between me and Dad in a coffee shop so he could answer all of my questions but we never got there. Instead we ended up following Mr "Maybe he's got a gun" when Dad recognised him.

Why this is important has just been added to the long list of questions I need to ask Dad.

Questions like,

Why did you leave?

Where have you been?

Why have you come back?

Oh, and I forgot.

Why are we following a man with a gun?

That one has sort of made it back to the top of the list now I've stopped shaking.

Before I can get started, Dad comes up with a couple of questions of his own, asking how come I'm so good at staying silent and how did I learn to follow someone like that?

I get away with saying I learned it from a book on spying which is such a lie if you know me.

It's a lie because firstly I'd need to find a spy book with lots of pictures and then I'd need to find someone to help me with the difficult words which for me means most of them.

You see, me and reading don't get on.

My teacher Miss S says I've got a sort of disease which scrambles my brain when I try to read and makes things difficult so it's not really my fault.

By the way, I also know that lying is wrong but sometimes it's got to be done.

I mean, I can't tell Dad all about the Red Sock Ninjas and about Kiera and about all the trouble we've nearly got into because that's all meant to be a big secret.

I also can't tell him because Red would kill me, which she wouldn't do really because she's my best friend. Another reason she wouldn't do it is because Keira would already have killed me and chopped up the bits to feed to angry badgers.

 Keira's like that.

 I know all of this sounds complicated but it's not really when compared to my life in general.

 Three coffees and two milkshakes later and I think I'm a bit wiser.

 I now know that Mum and Dad really have split up and that Dad is only here because Mum has suddenly decided that she needs a long rest. Actually, her doctor decided it for her and she's not really up to arguing at the moment.

 So, Dad has reappeared to look after me until he can sort something out.

 This is where it gets a bit fuzzy.

 I've never really understood what Dad does for a job and he's never talked about it much, even when we were a proper family. Back then he used to have to go away on business but he never brought back any presents.

I've figured out that he doesn't do a normal job.

That's unless I can think of any normal job which might end up with you being chased by men with guns.

Maybe Dad sells guns and our mystery man is a grumpy customer.

No, I don't believe it either.

Time I asked a few more questions.

Peter Marney

## My new Uncle

Have I told you my teacher can read minds?

Miss S always knows when something's not right with one of us in class. She doesn't say but I notice that sometimes she's extra kind if any of us are having a bad time.

She just seems to be able to work it out before the news runs around the playground so she's got to be able to read minds; there's no other explanation.

She also has this look which she gives you.

A worried look.

A bit like the one she's giving me right now.

I'm used to getting this look and it could mean all sorts of things.

She could be worried about my reading or my latest test results or about what Mr Ellis is going to say following his last visit. I get to see him when he comes into school because I read like a five year old, or maybe it's a six year old now as I've had a birthday.

Anyway, there's lots of reasons for Miss to be worried about me including the real reason which I hope she doesn't ask about yet until Wally and Red have worked out our story.

Why do I need a story?

Well, telling Miss about me and Dad's game of Hide and Seek with the gunman might ruin her day and lead to all sorts of other questions I'd rather not answer.

The bell goes for playtime and I think I've got away with it.

"Jamie, I need a word please."

Maybe not.

"I'm sorry to hear about your Mum Jamie."

How'd she know so quickly?

Mind reading!

"I hope she gets better soon and don't worry too much about homework. I'm sure your uncle has more than enough to do without trying to work out our maths problems."

Uncle?

"If you need anything or want to have a quiet talk anytime, then just let me know. All right?"

Uncle?

She even gives me a hug before I can escape to the playground.

Things must be worse than I thought.

I give Red our secret sign and she manages to stop playing with Naz and drifts over for a chat.

"Seems I've got a new uncle" I tell her.

This is sort of a good thing because new uncles aren't unusual on the estate.

Red explains that it usually means that some Mum's got a new boyfriend which in my case is so wrong in lots of ways.

If my Mum has got herself a new boyfriend then he must be really rubbish because she's decided not to stick around and instead has gone somewhere for a complete rest which means she's sort of sick.

Wally joins us and decides that Dad could be an uncle who's come to look after me while Mum is away. We don't need to explain why she's away because that's already old news if even Miss S knows about it.

Another reason for making up this story is because Dad has explained that he's sort of hiding at the moment. His job is something to do with finding out stuff and for some months he's been pretending to be someone else who's job definitely isn't about finding out stuff from the people he's now supposed to be friends with.

If they find out who he really is then it could be dangerous for all of us so I'd rather have a new uncle than meet our friend with the gun again.

By the way, Wally and Red are also Red Sock Ninjas and so it makes sense to tell them everything. We've nearly been in so much trouble together that, if they can't keep a secret, I'm dead anyway.

Besides, Wally is great at working out stuff and Red helps me understand things when they get a bit difficult.

That's what friends are for.

Now all I've got to do is find a way to explain it all to Keira and find a way to explain Keira to Dad.

This turns out not to be the problem I thought it would be.

When I get home from school, Keira is already there and cooking dinner.

The kitchen and me are both in shock.

Nobody has ever cooked a real meal in this kitchen since we moved in and Keira cooking??!

I can imagine her going out and slaying a dinosaur for dinner or maybe fighting a dragon but doing normal things like shopping and cooking just doesn't seem right.

Turns out there are some normal things that Keira doesn't do which is why I've now got my hands in this sink scrubbing the plates clean.

I'm also bringing Keira up to date on the various lies that have been told which now apparently includes her being a normal babysitter. Somehow she forgot to mention to Dad the bits about her being a Kung Fu expert and Red Sock Ninja Clan leader which is why he's happy to leave her in charge while he goes off in search of our missing friend.

This man is important as lots of people have been looking for him and Dad will make his boss happy if he can find out where he's been hiding; the man that is, not Dad's boss Mr Williamson although he's probably hiding somewhere as well.

Between you and me, I think my Dad's a spy.

That's why we've decided to help.

After all, five pairs of eyes are better than one and we can spread out further and search the whole town.

The only problem is that Red and Wally don't know what our gunman looks like. I can describe him really well because my memory is a bit like that unless it's anything to do with words and things.

Pictures, objects, people, I can remember.

Words, forget it.

What is it with me and words?

Oh, and I'm rubbish at drawing as well which is why Red is laughing at my piece of paper.

"Shame you can't tell your computer what to draw" she says.

Now that would be good.

"Imagine just talking to your computer and getting it to do what you want."

I'm already thinking about flying machines and talking computers so I guess I must have misheard Wally.

I thought he said,

"You can."

Then the bell goes and we're back to class.

"Look" says Wally, picking up my school tablet computer.

He presses a couple of buttons and then just talks to it while the screen fills up with words.

"Wow!"

Maybe that was a bit too loud. Miss S is coming over.

Wally has to explain what we're doing and then Miss tells us both to stay in after class.

I think we're in trouble.

Peter Marney

# Baby ninja

I know Miss has told me that she doesn't know everything but I've never really believed her. I mean, she's a teacher and a grown up.

Well, almost a grown up.

Sometimes she's just as silly as us.

Take now for instance.

Wally is busy talking to my computer, it's busy writing on its screen and I'm busy watching Miss do her Happy Dance around the classroom.

Don't worry, we're used to it by now.

When Miss is really pleased about something, she does this special dance.

"This is fantastic. Why didn't I know it could do this? Wally, can it read the words back to us as well? Just think what we can do with this Jamie. How do you get it to do all this Wally?"

I think she's excited.

Then I hear this strange computer voice reading back Wally's words and me and Miss both say "Wow!" together.

It's about now that I lose my computer.

Miss is going to take it home and play with it which is so not fair because she never lets me do that. I'm not even allowed to take it into the playground.

Me and Wally are now late for lunch but nobody shouts at us. I think I'm still getting special treatment because of Mum.

We're also late into the playground and have to search for Red.

She's with Naz as usual and is still laughing at my drawing skills or complete lack of them.

Naz is still the new girl in school and although we all get on ok, she doesn't know anything about the Red Sock Ninja Clan. This makes the explanation about my drawing difficult but I just say that the man I'm trying to draw is a friend of my uncle.

Turn's out we're not the only ones with secrets.

Naz has kept it quiet in class but she can draw. Not draw as in making it onto the Year Six display wall but draw as in "make it look like a photo" according to Red.

Naz doesn't do it in school because she says she just wants to fit in and not be special. Apparently having two Mums is more than enough to explain without Naz being this fantastic artist as well.

It sort of makes sense which is why we're now crowded around Naz's kitchen table while I close my eyes and give her the description of "my uncle's friend".

Naz starts to put his face on paper but it's a bit wonky.

"How wonky, Jamie? Which bits are wrong?"

I look carefully at the drawing and compare it to the picture in my head.

We then have this sort of tennis match where I say something and Naz redraws a bit of the picture. Then it's my turn again and we keep going until I don't have to say anything because Naz has got the image almost perfect.

This is the man we need to find.

Except that we don't.

Naz sees him every week when her Mums take her to church.

She even knows his name.

I wonder if he takes his gun to church?

We then spend ten minutes persuading Naz that it's not a good idea to tell Mr Andrews about his being a friend of her friend's uncle.

I never knew how good a liar Red can be when she really tries. Even I'm convinced by her story and I know that none of it's true.

Red doesn't like lying to Naz and tells us on the way home.

"She's my friend, almost like you two, and it's not right to lie to your friends is it?"

She's not wrong but I can't see a way to make it right.

"She's a good fighter too. You've seen her in the gym Jamie, she can almost beat me."

True.

You need to be a good boxer to beat Red.

"So, why can't she be a ninja as well?"

For some reason, my legs have stopped walking.

It's a good question.

But it's wrong.

She can't be a Red Sock Ninja. It's simple.

"Why not?"

I hate it when Red keeps asking good questions.

There's a whole room full of why nots but they all sort of come down to the same thing.

Keira.

Even though Red thought up the name and even though I'm the original Red Sock Ninja, it still all sort of comes down to what Keira thinks.

She's the leader, the best fighter and the one who plans most of our adventures. She's also the one who knows friends who can do all sorts of illegal things like break into computers and find us spy cameras.

Keira's a bit complicated.

She's not normal.

Well, I guess you've sort of worked that out for yourself.

She's also the one making sure that I stay fed and clean at the moment so there's quite a few reasons why I don't want to upset her.

We did have another member of the Red Sock Clan for a while but then Matt went back home to Poland and we went back to being just the original three of us, and Keira of course.

Why am I surrounded by grumpy females?

On the one hand I have Keira who could kill me and on the other I have Red who I think is getting angry with me.

This is not a good place to be.

I don't want to upset either of them.

"If you don't ask her then I will."

Wally?

Wally just said that?

"It does sort of makes sense Jamie, and we could do with someone else. Mum wants me to spend more time with Milly so I can't always be around and it'd be useful if Naz could sort of slot in when I'm missing."

I suppose that would be better than have Wally drag his little sister along. A baby ninja isn't something you see in the films and having Milly's special skills of missing her mouth with a spoon and producing stinky nappies isn't really something we're looking for in a new ninja.

Now all I've got to do is tell Keira.

Peter Marney

# Our new recruit

I'm getting the feeling that people aren't telling me things.

Dad has completely accepted Keira as my sitter who also happens to teach me judo at school and take me to boxing at the local youth club.

He thinks she's good for me!

So much for him being this amazing spy if he can't even work that out.

Maybe he really does do something boring for a job.

Anyway, I get to chat to Keira about Naz as we jog on our way to boxing. Well, most of it is jogging but we're also now running on some of the flat bits.

Keira thinks it's a good idea provided we only let Naz get involved in the semi-legal stuff, like following people and not like breaking into buildings. So I guess that Naz will be staying back after school judo in the future to help tidy up and practise ninja skills.

The next problem is how to tell her she's been accepted into a secret clan she knows nothing about. Perhaps I'll leave that one to Red. After all, it was her idea in the first place.

Keira got me started with boxing because I wasn't very good at judo and because I fought like a little girl, unless that little girl is Red. She fights like a teenaged boy who's just had his computer games nicked and who's taken a dose of extra strong grumpy medicine.

Big Jay, who runs the boxing, didn't like girls fighting but Keira changed his mind by dumping him on his bum with a kung fu kick and now they're friends and we've got Red and Naz and some other girls training with us.

Naz is getting as scary as Red and it's difficult to say who is the better fighter in the ring where they have rules.

In any other scrap I'd pick Red every time because she knows a few dodgy tricks like biting and can even beat her brothers if they're daft enough to get her angry and not run away.

Running away is always the best option though.

Shame I can't do that now.

For some reason, Red has persuaded her cousin Jay to let us fight and now she's trying to take my head off with a few swinging punches.

I think she's angry with me for some reason.

I manage to get close enough to grab her and, before she can start hitting my body, I whisper that "Keira says it's ok".

That stops the attack and Red starts dancing about on her feet and just jabbing at me. She knows she can beat me and so do I, which is why I'm now playing the game and pretending to try and hit her.

I do manage to get a few punches to land but I don't put any power behind them just in case I hurt her, or even worse, upset her. Even Jay gets out of the way when Red loses it.

During the break I ask Red to tell Naz the good news and she agrees to do it on Saturday when they go shopping together.

What is it with girls and shopping?

What are they shopping for anyway? New boxing gloves with matching handbags for their gum shields?

Dad hasn't been around long enough to tell him about church but the Red Socks are going to be outside on Sunday to follow our new mystery friend and see what happens.

I wonder if I should mention the gun to them?

Would it help do you think?

I decide to talk to Dad about Sunday when I get home but he's not there so Keira makes sure that I shower and brush my teeth before going to bed. Honestly, it's worse than having a proper Mum.

Over breakfast Dad looks worried so I tell him the good news about finding the mystery man but it doesn't cheer him up much. It's no good just finding this man; Dad needs to find out where he goes to in case it's the missing headquarters of the gang.

Didn't know we were up against a gang and still don't know what all this is about. What I do know is that people need to start telling me things.

Dad is worried about being spotted as they know his face so it seems a good idea to sort of tell him about how good me and my mates are at following people. I pretend it's a game we play.

This gives him the idea that we might follow the man after church on Sunday if we're careful. Why didn't I think of that?

Yes, I know I did think of that but I don't want Dad to know that because he might start asking the sort of questions that I don't want to answer.

We agree that me and my friends will do the following and that Dad will keep in the background and only get involved if there's trouble. That's normally Keira's job but she can't be involved at all without Dad getting the right idea about her and her role with the Red Sock Ninjas.

Keira does later approve the plan and gives us a briefing on the layout of the church and the area.

"Two ways out of the church but most people come out of the front door. Naz, you can be our eyes inside and if he looks to go out the other way then come out and signal us."

I don't know what Red told her but Naz has fitted in well and acts like it's all normal.

We agree that I'll take the lead with Red as back up and Wally across the road and also watching the other exit. If our man goes out that way then Wally takes the lead and we catch up.

I do have one question though.

"What do you wear for church?"

Peter Marney

# Spotted

How to be spotted in one easy lesson.

Stand outside a church and wait for someone to appear.

Which is exactly what we're not doing.

Instead, I'm waiting on the next corner with Red on the other corner by the side of the church and Wally by the rear exit. Dad is sitting in his car near me and ready to follow if needed.

When they all come out of church, I see our man chat to some people before walking down the road towards Red. She's already seen him coming and has disappeared down a side road and out of sight.

Luckily there's lots of people leaving church so I can just merge into the background and head off in the same direction while Wally and Red get into position.

At the shops, our man stops to look in the window which is a trick I use when I don't want to turn around and stare at someone. Either he already knows he's being followed or he's being very careful.

I just keep walking but signal those behind me to be careful as well. It's not me waving my arms in the air or anything, just a scratch of my bum like any normal kid would do. The Red Socks have lots of secret signs.

I'm getting a bit close to him now but I'm just staring down at the ground as usual and barely notice him as I pass which is just as well because he's now decided to go back the way he came.

This is really awkward if you're following someone by yourself but we're ready for him and both Red and Wally are out of sight and waiting to see what he does next.

On the basis that he's looking for any followers my job is finished. He'll have already noticed me and will realise it's me if I turn up later in the journey. All I can do is carry on walking until I can find a good reason to stop, like a bus stop or something.

That's why I miss the next bit but I find out later that he stopped and took a phone call before then starting to follow me, or at least head in the same direction. By then, I'd found my bus stop and am stood waiting in the queue pretending to read my comic when he comes towards me followed by Red and Wally.

If the bus arrives now I'll have to get on which could be a bit awkward as I don't have any money.

The man stops right next to me and reaches into his pocket.

Is this where I get shot?

I feel a poke in my back.

"What you doing here?"

I turn and look up.

It's Keira.

"I thought we were supposed to meet at half eleven. Did I get it wrong?"

The man has taken out his phone again and has started walking away.

"Smile Jamie" she whispers "and tell me I'm late."

I do, and we keep chatting while our target and his followers drift off.

Now the big question is, has he spotted me as a follower or just someone who he happened to see earlier.

If I was already out of the game, I'm even more dead now. There's no way he's not going to recognise me if I turn up again.

This guy has definitely got something to hide.

That something turns out to be very dull indeed as Red and Wally discover.

I see it later when Dad drives by and it's just a normal house. Hardly the secret lair we were expecting and Dad is disappointed.

"Ok, we've found where he lives but that's not much use and he's on the lookout for followers which means we can't use the same trick again. So not a good result Jamie is it?"

I agree but then I remember something Keira once told me.

"You've got to be the last one anybody suspects of being a ninja. Like in the films. The hero is always pretending to be a servant or a lowly wanderer. He doesn't come into town making a huge noise does he?"

It got me thinking.

"Dad, do secret enemy headquarters have a big sign over the door?"

"No, of course not Jamie."

He hasn't worked it out yet.

"So, without a sign, it could look just like any normal house then."

Dad starts smiling. I think he's getting the idea.

"I mean, it doesn't need lasers or lots of satellite dishes does it? A normal computer and phone could be all that's needed."

Dad nods.

He's definitely got the idea now.

"Might put in an alarm system though Jamie. Nothing too showy, but something to keep burglars away."

Not the burglars I'm thinking of. We know someone who's good with alarm systems.

Now all I've got to do is persuade Dad to let us break the law and break in.

Peter Marney

# Surprise

There's no way around it. I'm going to have to tell Dad about the Red Sock Ninjas.

I'm also going to have to explain Keira or at least get her to explain herself.

How else am I going to get permission to break the law?

I can't just do it without telling him. I think he might get a bit upset about me charging into someone's home. Especially someone who just happens to own a gun and probably isn't too worried about using it.

It's not all bad news though.

Miss has worked out how Wally got my computer to listen and talk to me so now I can get it to read the worksheets Miss has loaded onto it. I can also speak out my replies which makes everything a whole lot easier now that Miss doesn't have to struggle with my writing and my bad guesses at spelling.

I still have to do reading and writing but only in those lessons.

"History should be about history Jamie, not whether you can read the worksheets."

Now I can keep up with the rest of the class and join in with my own ideas. This is fantastic.

I even get permission to stay in at break time so that I can finish what I was doing in lessons. I'm on page four which is three and a half pages more than I usually manage.

Miss jokes that I'm giving her more work to do but I can see she's pleased.

That's when she suggests I should write stories.

"You've got a great imagination Jamie and if you don't have to struggle with spelling then you can just tell a story. You can talk it out to your computer and it can do the spelling for you."

I'm not sure. It sounds sort of difficult just making up things.

"If it's really good I can put it in the school competition if you like."

No pressure then.

Suddenly I'm turning from the kid who writes in rubbish to a master story teller.

"Maybe you could write about ninjas. You like ninjas don't you Jamie?"

Miss seems very keen on the idea so I agree if only to shut her up.

As if I don't have enough problems already.

At least I have an excuse to leave Naz out of our raiding party. It might make church a bit awkward for her and her Mums if we get caught.

Not that we intend to get caught. This is going to have to be a very well planned operation.

Time for Wally.

If you don't know Wally you might think he's a bit on the slow side. It's not that he doesn't understand; he understands too much.

While we can see maybe one or two answers, Wally can find at least a dozen more and is busy thinking about what's the best one while the rest of us are carrying on with the conversation and have forgotten the original question.

But for a well thought out plan, Wally is your ninja.

He's also found this program on the computer which is like a spy in the sky. It can even see into my garden although I think it uses old pictures unless I've got a swing I don't know about.

Anyway, we've got a birds eye view of our target house and garden.

Red is going to take a crash course in alarm systems from one of her uncles who thinks she's interested in home security. He's sort of right but Red's interest is more about home insecurity.

Me?

I've got the easy job of telling Keira what we've planned and getting her to help me convince Dad.

I have had one good idea though.

I think I might do a story about the Red Sock Ninjas. I won't call them that of course and I won't use our real names or say what we look like but I think the stories might be fun to read.

Maybe I'll just try one out on Miss and see what she thinks.

Now to my other problem.

"Dad, how do you feel about me breaking into these secret headquarters, you know, just to check we've got the right building?"

No, perhaps that's a bit blunt.

"Dad, you know you said we should do more things together? How about we break in to this house with a few of my mates?"

Not any better is it.

Maybe I'll just make something up as it happens.

I am so clueless.

I couldn't be more clueless if I'd just dropped a whole box of clues into a bottomless pit which sucked them into another dimension where a black hole gobbled them up and sent them into infinity to be eaten by angry star dogs.

That night when I get home, Dad is sitting there with Keira.

"Jamie, we need to talk."

Ok, I'm definitely in trouble about something.

Still clueless though but now on a whole new level.

"We need to tell you something."

We?

Oh no, they're not getting married are they?

Having a new uncle is bad enough, I don't want a new Mum as well and especially not one who can kick my head off if she gets mad at me.

"You know I've been working undercover Jamie?"

I nod.

"Well, it made sense to make sure you and Mum were protected as well. That's why you had to suddenly move here."

Oh, there was a reason then. Mum never said.

"I couldn't be here to look after you, so I made sure that someone kept an eye on you."

Why are they smiling?

What's so funny?

Seems like a perfectly sensible idea. Get someone to give Mum a call now and then and check that nobody with a gun has been knocking at the door. Maybe call round occasionally and check out the bushes for invaders.

They must be good though, because I've never spotted them although I do think that milkman we had at Christmas was a bit too friendly.

"Who was it Dad? Have I met him?"

Now they're laughing.

I'm definitely missing a joke somewhere which isn't unusual for me. I'm not very good with jokes.

"Not him Jamie."

If not him then it must be a her.

Maybe he had a word with Miss S and she's been keeping a special eye on me. Maybe...

Oh.

If it's not Miss S then it's got to be...

Oh.

Peter Marney

# A family outing

Well, that explains a lot of things.

Keira isn't Keira at all.

Well, she is and she isn't.

She's still the same scary babysitter and Red Sock Ninja Clan leader and I've still got to call her Keira but she's not really any of that because she's something else.

Something else and a lot more.

All these secrets I was trying to keep from Dad and he knows about it already because Keira or whatever she's really called has been keeping him up to date.

Seems that it's only me who isn't up to date.

There I was, worried about how to tell Dad about Keira and the Red Sock Ninjas and now all I've got to do is work out how to tell the Red Sock Ninjas about Keira.

"So Jamie, how are we going to break into this house we've found?"

Well, that solves that problem. Dad's not worried about me risking my life against armed men then.

I tell both of them what we've worked out so far and from the way they're nodding it seems like Wally has done a good job with the plan.

Red doesn't need the crash course though as Dad will be coming with us and alarms won't be a problem.

I think this means that he also knows a bit about home insecurity.

Keira and Wally will guard the outside exits while me, Red and Dad find out what's inside.

Naz has already told me that our Mr Andrews is always at the Sunday church service so that becomes our window of opportunity to slide though. I just hope that the vicar has a long sermon to give this week.

Daytime ninja work is a bit different from the usual.

Normally I'd be wearing my dark hoodie and black trainers and a special mask which makes me not me.

Now, I'm just the usual forgettable boy who's being lifted over the back garden fence and into more bushes.

Why do I always end up in the bushes?

Everything is quiet, so I knock on the fence and two more people join me in bush heaven.

I guess being an enemy agent doesn't leave too much time to do the gardening. Everything is overgrown which is good for us as it gives us plenty of hiding space.

Dad has taken out a small pair of binoculars and is busy carefully looking at the back of the house and especially the windows.

There's a very attractive window upstairs but that would mean climbing up onto the extension roof where it's just so easy to wave at any nosy neighbour who happens to wander into their garden.

As we really don't want to be noticed by neighbours, we slide across to one of the extension's small windows so that Dad can fiddle with its catch.

When it opens, there isn't much of a gap but it's wide enough for a small girl to wriggle through and open the big window for the rest of us to climb through which now puts us out of sight of the neighbours and into enemy territory.

Dad does a quick look around the ground floor and discovers absolutely nothing. No alarms, no secret spy centre, and nothing of interest at all.

Upstairs is a bit different though.

Inside one of the small bedrooms we find a very nice computer and a very locked filing cabinet. Red is looking at its lock when I notice a couple of wires coming out of the back.

That's when Dad tells us to freeze.

I think these wires might mean something. Something like please leave me alone unless you want me to blow up the whole building with you still inside.

Maybe the computer will be a bit friendlier.

Maybe not.

Now what do you think would be a good password for an enemy agent?

"World Control"?

No.

"Superspy"?

No.

Red searches the bookcase while I look in the drawers of the desk in case, like most people, he's written down his password somewhere.

Why does a spy need so many books?

This is a good question apparently because Dad takes out this small camera and takes a picture of the bookcase.

"I'll explain later Jamie."

Oh good, at last someone's going to start telling me stuff.

While he's busy getting the bookcase to smile for the camera I fiddle with the keyboard.

"QWERTY"

No, that doesn't work.

"123456"

No, it doesn't like that either.

Suddenly I get an idea.

"Pa55w0rd"

Who's a clever boy then?

Or rather, who's a really stupid spy? Why does everyone think that swapping a few letters for numbers will make their password secure?

Even I stopped using "Pa55w0rd" once Keira told me how stupid it was.

Dad takes over and searches the emails.

He's going too quick for me to read anything but to be fair a tortoise can move too fast for me when it comes to reading emails.

Shame this isn't one of those computers which reads aloud to you.

Dad is going really fast. How can he do that?

Red is keeping an eye on the time and Naz is going to text as soon as the service is over which might be that quiet buzz which has just come from Red's phone.

Three minutes to get out of church, a couple of minutes chatting, and then say six minutes to walk home. We'll need at least five minutes to get out of here and maybe a bit longer to make sure that everything is tidy.

Dad has found some maps with crosses marked on them.

"This is it Jamie, quick, take a photo of the screen."

I take two, just to be sure, and try not to shake and make it blurry.

Red tells us it's time to go just as Dad finds a special file.

"It's names Jamie, lots of names, addresses and stuff."

He starts scrolling down the list really fast. The list goes on forever.

Then he goes back and does a page at a time but still really quick.

Red is waving her wrist at me and pointing to her watch.

Another buzz from Red's pocket.

"The text says Billy's got a cold" Red whispers.

This is a code.

It means that Mr Andrews is at the top of the road and will be home very soon.

Dad still hasn't finished reading the list but we really do need to be somewhere else really really quickly.

I press the power down button.

"Out of time Dad. We're leaving. Now!"

We carefully haven't moved anything so there's not much to double check. Quickly, we're down the stairs and out to the extension.

This time we're all out of the main window which I close while Dad lifts up Red to wriggle through and push down the main catch. As she slides back to the ground Dad fiddles the latch closed on the little window as somewhere a door slams.

This is not a good sound.

Red is first over the wall with Dad giving her a boost up. I'm to follow but there isn't time.

That's why we're back in the bushes again.

Back trying to be silent while Mr Andrews takes a walk in his overgrown garden.

# Code and chips

What's the first thing you do when you get back home?

Take your coat off and put the kettle on?

No.

Every good spy knows that the first thing you do is take a stroll around your garden.

Maybe he's thinking about today's sermon or doesn't want to be inside on such a nice day.

I don't want to be inside either.

Not inside this bush or inside this garden.

What we need now is a good diversion.

Something to take this nice man's mind off of overgrown grass and dead flowers.

Thank you Keira.

At least that's who I'm assuming has set off the car alarm which Mr Andrews is suddenly interested in investigating.

One, two, three, four.

Give him time to reach the door.

Five, six, seven , eight.

Over the fence before it's too late.

Not my best poem ever, but you get the idea of the next hurried minute.

That was far too close for my liking and I hope whatever Dad was reading was worth the delay and possible capture.

If I'm going to get shot then I'd like to know it was for a good cause.

All we've got to do now is look like a normal family out for a Sunday stroll to the park where we can have some fun.

Who knows, we might even meet up with a few friends who also happen to think that a trip to the park on a nice day is a good idea.

We say hello to Keira and Wally as we pass their park bench and then start to make our way home, happy that we've all got away from the house safely.

Plan completed.

We've already agreed that the Red Socks should keep away from my house for a while, just in case, so I'll be reporting back on what we found when I get back to school on Monday morning.

For now, me and Keira are clearing a space on the table for when Dad brings in the take away.

I tell her all about the filing cabinet and the computer and my good question about the bookshelf.

I don't often get things right so I might as well mention it when I do.

Dad's now back so we continue to talk over mouthfuls of fish and chips and for once I don't get told off for speaking with my mouth full of food.

"What do you know about codes Jamie?" Dad asks.

I suppose the answer is lots and nothing.

Lots because nearly all the words I read seem to be in code, and nothing because, well, code and normal look the same to me.

He starts to explain but soon picks up from my blank look that he might as well be talking in code rather than trying to explain about it. So he starts again.

"A good quick code can either use letters or numbers."

Ok so far.

"Or you can mix the two like in your 'Pa55w0rd'."

Yes, I can understand that.

"But you need to be able to decode as well so whatever method you use has got to work both ways."

I'm getting worried, this is still making sense.

"Now, if I said 53,9,4,2 what do you think that might mean?"

That's better. Now I'm back to being clueless.

"It might mean the letter A" he explains.

All that for one letter? No wonder spies don't write stories.

"You see, if two spies use the same version of a book, then this code makes sense. Page 53, line 9, choose the fourth word on that line, and the second letter of that word. A."

Ah, now I understand, sort of.

Keira joins in.

"All you've got to do is find the exact book they're using and then, when you intercept the message, you can work out the code."

The bookshelf!

I decide to join the conversation, despite having a mouth full of chips.

"MMghf wwmpf"

Ok, maybe I'll swallow first.

"But there were lots of books. It'll take ages to get copies of

the exact same books and which ones
do you choose? The code could be in
any of them."

Dad's plugged his small camera
into Keira's computer.

"Look at the titles Jamie" she
says.

I give Keira a look instead. At
least she should remember my secret
non-skill.

"Oh, sorry Jamie, I forgot. Let me
tell you then. Lots of cookery
books, some stories, a book on
gardening, and a couple of books on
local history. Where do you think
we should start?"

Well, if I could read then I'd
want some cookery books to help
make food interesting, and it might
be useful to know about round here
if you come from somewhere else. I
don't know anything about growing a
garden so that book on gardening
would be really useful.

Really useful if I did any gardening.

Or did anything other than just walk around my garden on a Sunday after church.

They both agree with me that the gardening book makes a good first choice for the enemy spy code.

That's why Dad is now emailing his boss Mr Williamson with details of what he's been up to and what he's found.

"Best to keep you lot out of this for now" he says "I'll just tell him what he needs to know and no more. Always a good idea to keep some secrets."

I think so too.

That's why I'm only telling Miss about our walk in the park when she asks what we all did over the weekend.

I'm going to keep my deeds about saving the world for my story about the Green Tiger Ninjas.

I hope my computer can understand the word ninja.

Now we just wait for Dad's boss to organise a raid on the house and capture the enemy spy.

What could possibly go wrong?

Peter Marney

# Parklife

The trouble with keeping the Red Sock Ninjas away from my house is what do I do after school?

The invisible swing in the garden has still failed to show itself and there's only so many films you can watch before you know the words better than the actors.

I've been thinking about my story and have lots of ideas for Green

Tiger adventures. The only trouble is that Miss S will recognise a lot of what might be in the stories and I'd rather she didn't know about some of it. Actually I'd rather she didn't know about any of it or else she might go searching for a green tiger and find a red sock.

If you've been looking for someone for a while and really wanted to talk to them then you'd think that finding them would be a good thing wouldn't you?

Mr Williamson doesn't seem to think so.

He's told Dad to tell nobody about any of this and wants to meet him urgently tomorrow in our local park.

That's why I'm standing at the bottom of a tree holding a camera on a string while Wally is finding somewhere high up to fix it to a branch. It's nice and dark at the moment and, with the park gates locked, nobody should disturb us.

We've already got one other spy camera in place and Red is working with Keira with the last of the three. Between them, we should be able to get a good overall view of the meeting.

Dad's busy at home on Keira's computer copying down all of the contact details he read on the spy machine. Turns out his memory's even better than mine and is something he calls photographic. This means that he can use his memory as a camera which is a bit like what I can do with objects and people but his works with words as well.

When we get home, he's printed several sheets of paper covered with writing.

"It's not just names Jamie, there's addresses and numbers and other marks as well."

I thought it was just a list of enemy agents but Dad says that some of the names are people he knows and others have turned out to be just ordinary people picked at random.

I think that some of them must be spies but nobody would be daft enough to have a list of secret members on their computer would they?

"Where's the best place to hide a leaf Jamie?"

Keira sounds like one of those monks in a kung fu film.

A secret underground safe surrounded by a pool of man eating sharks?

No, you'd have to keep visiting to feed the fish.

Ok, I know they're not fish but you know what I mean.

Maybe you could tuck the leaf into the pages of a book and hide the book in a huge library filled with loads of other books.

"Good idea Jamie, but what if someone picked up the book by accident? Rather an unusual place to find a leaf isn't it? Must be an important leaf maybe."

Hmm, hadn't thought of that.

Where wouldn't a leaf stick out?

I've got it!

"In a bush. You hide it in a bush with lots of other leaves which all look the same."

But what's all of this got to do with a list of names?

Got it again!

I must be having one of my clever Jamie days.

You hide the special names in with a load of normal names and have some code for saying who is who. All we've got to do is work out what the code word or mark is.

Dad deletes the file on Keira's computer and then sends her home with a copy of the printed list to hide somewhere safe.

"Always good to have a back up plan Jamie."

Funny, that's one of Keira's sayings as well.

Our back up plan involves those cameras busy pretending to be leaves.

Next morning I'm too sick to go to school and will be spending the day in bed. At least, that's what Dad's just said on the phone to them.

Really, I'm sitting in the back seat of his car watching over his shoulder as he looks at a computer screen showing what our cameras are seeing.

"See anything unusual Jamie?"

A test.

The park seems to be busy this morning with a couple of mums gossiping on a bench and a few dog walkers. Someone else is out jogging and there's a chap taking pictures of bushes for some reason. Good job our cameras are a bit higher.

The problem with spotting something unusual is knowing what's normal for a park in the morning. If it were school, then I'd spot something out of place right away but who knows, maybe the bush snapper is always there.

"Nobody is talking Jamie, apart from the two women. People talk in parks even if it's only to say "Good Morning". Everybody seems too keen on ignoring each other."

He's right and something's wrong.

"If I was going to snatch someone Jamie, I'd put a couple of people on that bench to guard the way out, someone else to block the other exit, and a few mobiles to pick up the target when they appear."

How does he know this stuff?

He starts the car.

"Strap in Jamie, I think we need to be somewhere else."

On the way, Dad stops to make a call to his boss and gives an excuse for not making the park today, arranging instead to meet in town next week when he's over the flu.

At home we watch what happens in the park as the meeting time comes and goes. A couple of people glance at their watches and then slowly, about five minutes after Dad's phone call, the park empties.

Maybe they're all off to get a cup of coffee at the same time. Or maybe they're going to a meeting to find out why Dad suddenly cancelled his visit.

I think perhaps we'll have to disappear for a while and let Wally get the cameras back on his own tonight.

# Ducks

At home the radio tells us there's been a bomb set off in the city.

Dad is angry.

"That's one of the places I told them about on the map we saw. Why didn't they stop it? Why weren't they ready?"

He contacts a friend who he says does the same type of work. I think that means he's a spy too.

If these guys really are all spies then how come they've not traced Dad's mobile?

I'm getting good with these questions.

Dad explains that he's got a special phone which can't be traced because…

And there I got lost for a minute or two.

It sounded very technical though.

Dad's friend tells him that nobody knows anything about where the enemy targets might be and that they're still all looking for the secret headquarters.

All he knows is that Dad is on the wanted list for leaking information about their own double agents in the enemy team.

I've got another question.

"If your Mr Williamson has got agents working with the enemy, then why didn't he already know about these targets and about the headquarters, and about where to find Mr Andrews?"

Dad's been thinking the same thing and is trying to recall the list in his head again.

"Thomas, Thompson, Travis, Valcheck, Wall, Wallace."

That was the last name he read before I hit the power switch.

"Travis is one of ours Jamie, and I recognised some other names as well."

Maybe these are the secret double agents, but why would they use their real names? Aren't spies always supposed to use fake names? Even I know that.

None of this is making sense.

Keira pops round in the afternoon and we work out a plan for getting our cameras back. Dad won't let me out so Keira and Red will have to guard the exits while Wally goes tree climbing again.

At least that works out as planned although it took longer than we thought. Wally said that he got stuck in the last tree as some older kids nipped in over the fence and started messing around and kicking a bench to bits. Then one of them got a text message and they ran back over the fence again which gave Wally time to get down and out of the park just before Keira was about to go in to find him.

I start yawning while they're telling us what happened which is the sign for everyone to go home as we've all got school tomorrow.

Just before they leave, Keira tells us all about the film we've supposed to have been watching this evening. It's sort of something to do with our school projects which is always a good excuse for doing stuff.

Good job Keira knows a lot about films.

Maybe I could use one of those kung fu films for a story. That might make Miss happier than one of my made up things.

The next morning I find out that I chose a good day to be away.

The school story competition results were announced and there was a man from the paper and a photographer and everything. Mrs Wallace tells us all this in big assembly and all the winners are called out, including me for coming third in the Junior section.

If I'd been there yesterday, my face would have been in today's news. That was a lucky escape.

Miss is doing her happy dance again in class and everyone cheers.

Because of my story, the school is going to be getting some more of these computer tablets to help kids like me.

"See Jamie" says Miss, "I told you that you could write. You just needed some help from a talking computer."

I think Wally had something to do with it as well but he's got the same cold that I had yesterday and is probably sleeping in to make up for last night's wait in the treetops.

Now I suppose I'll have to start working even harder and Miss will be wanting some more stories as well.

At least she's happy though and doesn't use her worried look on me.

She would though if she knew half of the stuff that's going on at the moment.

My uncle, who's really my Dad, is really a spy and is chasing enemy spies while now being hunted by his own side. Some of these people probably have guns and some definitely have bombs.

Maybe I should just stick it all in a story and watch her face as she reads it. It scares me so I've no idea what it would do to her.

Wally's back for the afternoon and has some news.

He did sleep in late but then his Mum made him go with her and Milly for a walk in the park. I think Wally's getting fed up with that park by now.

Anyway, guess who he spots sitting on one of the non-broken benches chatting to someone?

Our Mr Andrews has found a friend.

Wally skips feeding the ducks with his family and instead sneaks into the bushes and into hearing range.

Mr Andrews is saying that the net is closing and that Blue Team must go into hiding. They're to meet there tonight when it's quiet and a van will collect them and go to the new safe house.

Wally didn't hear any more but is sounds like he's heard enough.

 If we act quickly we can catch the whole team together and at least get their photos or something. Shame Wally took down those cameras.

 I can't wait to get home and tell Dad.

## Ambush

It was all supposed to go so well.

Dad would sit in his car and watch one entrance while Keira would be at the other end of the park guarding that way in.

That left the three of us to find some good hiding places where we could take photos of Blue Team when they turned up.

The first problem was Milly, the baby ninja.

Measles.

Milly has got measles and Wally isn't allowed out tonight.

Normally, this should be where Naz steps in but neither Keira or Dad will let her come because it might be dangerous.

What about me and Red?

If it's dangerous then why are we being allowed to do it?

Keira's got a good answer for that one.

"Because you're Red Sock Ninjas and I've trained you."

Can't argue with that can I?

Actually, Keira's got two answers, and the other one is that she's going to be joining the team to replace Wally and to protect us if anything goes wrong.

Does she have a gun as well?

I don't think I want to know. Keira is scary enough without thinking of her with a loaded pistol.

Then there's the question of timing.

We've no idea when Blue Team is supposed to turn up and so we could be there all night.

Now you already know about my love of bushes but even I draw the line at standing in one for eight hours.

Dad's idea was that they won't leave it too late because a van driving around when the roads are completely empty will stand out a bit and the police might take an interest and stop it for a look inside.

So we agree to be in place and hiding before sunset and to stay there until midnight. Then the witches and vampires can take over.

I wish I hadn't said that.

Now I'm worried about vampires as well.

Yes, I know they don't exist but when it goes all dark and quiet and you've only got a bush for company then they might, sort of, possibly exist, just a bit, maybe.

Witches?

No, I don't need to be worried about them because I've got one hiding about three bushes away. At least, that's where I last saw Keira before she disappeared.

We don't know how many to expect tonight but I guess that a special team can't be that big. I'd keep it to four or five at the most so with Mr Andrews as well, I think we'll be taking snaps of about six people.

Well, it seems I'm right about that anyway.

Mr Andrews has just come into sight and, out of the far bushes, I can see four, no five figures emerging, all dressed in dark clothing.

But instead of all coming together to greet Mr Andrews, they start to spread out. Two head towards the far gate and another two back to where Dad is hiding with his car. It's only the last one who goes up to Mr Andrews and they stand there talking and pointing around the park.

This isn't how it's supposed to happen.

Still, I get a few long distance photos of them chatting and pointing, with one where they're almost looking right towards me. It would be a really good shot if they weren't wearing masks.

Silence.

I know there's at least eight other people in this park but I can't hear any of them. I'm hoping that the two pairs are just guarding the gates and not waiting for anyone else.

Maybe they don't know which exit the van is going to be using and so want to check both.

The only thing to do is stay in this bush and wait to see what happens.

If you're hiding then the worst thing you can do is start moving. For some reason movement seems to catch our eyes more than anything so it's one of the first things you learn in infants when you're playing hide and seek.

Don't move.

Especially don't move when you suddenly see an unexpected body walking up right by the bush which I hope is still keeping me hidden.

They're not guarding the exits; they're searching the park.

Why are they searching the park?

Maybe they're just being careful.

I'd be careful if I was having a secret meeting and I'd make sure that I wasn't being spied on by anyone.

The whole team are now back where they should be and none of us have been discovered. All of them have got masks on so there's no point in trying to take any more photos.

Why didn't we think of them wearing masks?

It's what we're doing so why not them?

Now they're splitting up again and I hope on their way to the van. Maybe we can get a photo of its number plate although I expect it's a false one or even a stolen van.

So much for good plans.

Well, at least we won't be here all night.

Suddenly there's someone else in my bush and I feel two arms grabbing round me and hauling me into the moonlight. I try to struggle but he's stronger and taller than me and he just lifts me off of the ground.

In the struggle he's ripped my hood off and so I can see two other fights going on.

The poor chap who grabbed Red is now calling for help while holding onto a ball of swinging arms, legs and feet all trying to find something to hit, scratch, or bite.

Keira has managed to floor her attacker with a kick but is now just standing there and doing nothing except look at me.

I suppose it's got something to do with the fact that Mr Andrews is now right next to me and pointing his gun at my head.

This is definitely not how the plan's supposed to work out.

# Disaster

Not a word has been said.

They've ripped off our hoods and taken photos of us but there have been no questions or threats.

Just silence.

We're being carefully walked towards the far gate and I'm afraid I've just worked out why they need a van.

It's not for Blue Team.

It's for us.

We're being kidnapped.

Red is looking like she wants to kill someone really soon but Keira is glaring at her which I think means "don't you dare". Even with Keira on our side, this is a fight we're never going to win.

It's one of Keira's sayings.

"Never enter a bum kicking contest with a porcupine because you're always going to lose."

The only way to win is find a bigger porcupine and I think the shops have all just sold out tonight.

Then suddenly it's not so silent any more.

I hear the noise of a car or something screeching away at speed and then the sound of police sirens. I can see blue lights flashing at both park entrances and can just make out the policemen getting out of their cars.

Before we can move, the Blue Team
are running with Mr Andrews towards
the fence they climbed in over and
we're left alone to face the
police.

The plan, if we got caught, was to
say that we were trying to catch
the vandals who broke our park
bench.

Time to see if it works.

It doesn't.

Not only don't the police believe
us, they think we're the vandals
and take us to the police station.
Someone saw us breaking into the
park and telephoned them so it must
be true.

We'd still be there if the vandals
hadn't struck themselves later that
night.

While we're being questioned,
someone set alight to two more park
benches and it needed the fire
brigade to put out the flames. I

wondered why Dad had put that can of petrol into the boot of his car.

 With the proof that we can't be setting fires and talking to policemen at the same time, our story is finally believed and we're set free after being firmly told to leave this sort of thing to the police.

 We might be free but we're not safe.

Blue Team and the enemy know what we look like and have photos as well. If they want us then it's not going to be too difficult to find us is it?

 Dad collects us from the police station.

 "Time to leave."

 I hope he means the police station but I know it's more than that.

 The only way we're going to stay safe is to run away.

 Run way and hide.

Go undercover.

All of us.

This is exactly what he means, but before we disappear there's one small job to be sorted out.

Wally.

Who was the one who said he'd overheard the enemy?

Wally.

Who helped us make our plans to spy on them?

Wally.

Who suddenly couldn't join us tonight?

Wally.

So, who must have told the enemy all about our plans?

The enemy have got to Wally and he's betrayed us to them.

Set us up in the park to be captured.

Well, now it's time to take revenge.

Red calls him on his mobile and says we've got the photos and need him to hide the cameras for us.

Why has everyone got a mobile except me?

If I live through this, I'm going to have a serious talk with Dad about mobiles.

We meet behind Wally's house and I can tell he knows.

Red doesn't say anything, she just thumps him right in the face.

Not once, not twice, but three times and he just stands there watching her doing it while she's crying at the same time.

He got caught trying to get our spy cameras out of the trees but they were clever.

Nobody was going to get hurt if they could capture us.

But if Wally didn't help them, then Milly would be having an accident some time soon.

He didn't have a choice.

Wally might be a Red Sock Ninja but he's also a big brother and big brothers are supposed to look after their little sisters.

So Wally isn't a Red Sock Ninja any more and he's being beaten up to make sure the enemy knows we've found out.

He's also being beaten up to make sure that the enemy doesn't know that Wally told us exactly what happened as soon as he got back from getting the cameras out of the park.

We knew we were walking into a trap but we had an escape route planned.

Ok, that plan didn't work but at least Wally didn't betray us and we can't betray him.

The enemy have got to be sure that we've worked out they got to Wally and that he's now paying the price.

That's why Red is hitting him and that's why she's crying.

None of us want do it but it's got to be done for his and Milly's safety before we run away. Wally can't run and Milly can't even walk yet so we had to find a way for them to safely stay behind and this is it.

Now for the bit of the plan where we run away like headless chickens with nowhere to hide.

Except we call it Plan C and we do have somewhere to hide.

It's a car ride away but it's only for one night.

That's the good news.

The bad news is that, after tomorrow, we're going to have to split up and I won't be staying with Red or Keira. Finding four people together is a lot easier than trying to find two pairs so it sort of makes sense.

We're not sure exactly what happens after tomorrow or how to explain our sudden departure and for once I'm glad I'm not a grown up. Dad and Keira can sort this one out.

It's sad to have to leave home and it's even sadder to have to leave friends but at least Wally will be safe now, even if he'll have a bruised face for a few weeks.

We all say goodbye to each other and then suddenly it's time to leave.

Time to leave home, school, friends, and my whole life.

We might be apart but we'll always be the Red Sock Ninja Clan.

That will last forever.

# The End

# The next book in the series

Where do you run to when everything goes wrong?

That's the latest problem for the Red Sock Ninjas and this time Wally isn't around to mastermind a clever plan.

Is this the end of the Clan or the beginning of a whole new experience for Jamie?

Peter Marney

# About the author

Peter Marney lives by the sea, is just as bad at drawing as Jamie, and falls over if his socks don't have the right day of the week written on them.

On a more serious note, Peter has worked supporting children with reading difficulties and understands some of their problems. He is passionate about the importance of both reading and storytelling to the growing mind.

Peter Marney

# The Red Sock Ninja Clan Adventures

## Birth of a Ninja

Jamie's about to start another new school and has been told to stay out of trouble. Like that's going to happen!

It's not as if he wants to fight but you've got to help out if a girl's being picked on, right? Even if it does turn out that she's the best fighter in the school and laughs at your odd socks.

Follow Jamie as he makes friends, sorts out a big problem at his school, and discovers that his weird new babysitter knows secret ninja skills.

# Hide and Seek

Find out why Jamie hates dogs and why he's hiding in a school cupboard in the dark. Has it got something to do with Keira's new training games for the Red Sock Ninjas?

## The Mystery Intruder

Someone is playing in school after dark and it's not just the Red Sock Ninjas. Maybe Harry knows who it is but he's not talking so Jamie will have to find another way to solve this mystery.

## The Mighty Porcupine

What do you do when your enemy is too powerful to fight? Has somebody finally beaten the Red Sock Ninjas?

## The Mystery Troublemakers

Someone wants to get Jamie's new youth club into trouble but why?

Maybe the Red Sock Ninjas can find the answer by climbing rooftops or will it just get them into more trouble?

# Statty Sticks

Why is Jamie being attacked by a small girl who isn't Red and why does he get the feeling that someone is spying on him?

Has it got anything to do with why his school is in danger and how numbers can lie?

# Enemies and Friends

Why has Jamie got a new uncle and why does everyone end up hiding in bushes?

Have the Red Sock Ninjas now found too big a porcupine and will it spell disaster for their future together?

# Run Away Success

Where do you run to when everything goes wrong? That's the latest problem for the Red Sock Ninjas and this time Wally isn't around to mastermind the plan.

With the enemy closing in for capture, the friends must split up and disappear. Is this the end of the Clan or the beginning of a whole new experience for Jamie?

# Rise and Shine

Why does going to the library get Jamie into a fight and what's that got to do with Keira's plan for getting rid of him?

Helping to put on a show with Miss G was difficult enough without guess who turning up. Yet again the Red Socks must use their skills to save the day and the show.

# Rabbits and Spiders

Has Red set up Jamie on a date with Dog Girl? If so, why is he now running around in circles? Maybe it's got something to do with the fact that the enemy have at last found them again.

The Red Sock Ninjas must use all of their skills in this last adventure if they are to escape and live happily ever after.

Printed in Great Britain
by Amazon

42609139R00073